The Should I? Game

Helen R. Letts

This book is a work of fiction.
Names, characters, places, and incidents are a
product of the author's imagination or are used
fictitiously. Any resemblance to actual persons,
living or dead, events, or locales is purely
coincidental.

Copyright © 2014 by Helen R. Letts
Cover design by Helen R. Letts

All rights reserved. No part of this book may be
reproduced, scanned, or distributed in any printed
or electronic form or by any means without the
express permission in writing from the author.

ISBN10: 0988933330
ISBN13: 978-0-9889333-3-0
Library of Congress Catalog Control Number
2014904593
Printed in the United States

Xbox® is a registered trademark of Microsoft
Corporation.

For Jace, Mia, Peyton, and Brody

CONTENTS

Acknowledgments	i
Saturday, 8 a.m.	1
Saturday, 8:30 a.m.	7
Saturday, 9 a.m.	33
Saturday, 9:30 a.m.	57
Saturday, 10 a.m.	75
Newbold Family Should I? List	81

ACKNOWLEDGMENTS

Many thanks to my enthusiastic young reviewers—Cassie Fuller, Cai Warner, and Kobe Warner—for their wonderful feedback, and to writer/editor Peter Delaney for his invaluable assistance. And gratitude to Carol, Heidi, Karen, Patsy, Lanny, and Shirley—friends and family who assumed the roles of reviewers and proofreaders—for the gift of their time.

SATURDAY, 8 A.M.

It wasn't the warm rays of the early morning sun peeking through the window blinds that woke him. Nor was it his sister, Sophia, talking loudly on the cell phone she had been given days before for her sixteenth birthday. No, it was Willy. Willy, the fat Blue Russian cat with eyes the color of amber and a coat the color of the steel wool his mother sometimes used to scrub metal pans. Willy was practically sitting on his face. The cat's purr was loud and rough and reminded him of the sounds made by stones tumbling in the cement mixer his father had used last year to extend the concrete patio at the back of the house.

Chance tried to push the cat away, annoyed that in his all-too-real dream he was about to lose his first place position in the race. He had just passed the halfway point in the last lap of the race, and was cruising toward the finish line at a speed in excess of 100 miles per hour, his hands gripping the wheel of the two-toned red 2009 Bugatti Veyron 16.4. The car was a sleek beauty, its engine powerful, and he could feel the high-velocity buzz of that power zipping through his body like bolts of electricity. He needed to finish the race, to claim his victory. He pressed the gas pedal a bit more and pushed again at the cat. The car zoomed forward, the cat didn't.

Willy's answer was to purr even louder and to begin rhythmically kneading and digging his claws into the side of Chance's head. When the cat's claws pierced his skin, Chance screamed and sat straight up in bed, clutching the side of his head where he was sure there now were puncture wounds, clawed trenches, and blood. Willy shot off the bed and escaped through the door flung open by Sophia who had sprinted across the hall to Chance's room when she heard him cry out as if—as she later described it to the family—he was being viciously attacked by some wild animal. As soon as she saw Willy streak past her and Chance's hand clutching the side of his head, Sophia knew exactly what had happened.

"Are you okay?" She stood in the doorway holding the phone in its bling case to her chest, her hair wrapped in a towel. Despite his pain, Chance couldn't stop the thought that popped into his head when he saw her. Sophia looked like she had a cone head.

"No," he snapped, his thick eyebrows were pinched together, forming a straight line above light blue eyes, darker than usual now as they reflected pain. He threw himself back against the pillow and said, "I had the lead, Soph...the lead! And I was in the last lap, ahead of everyone," he practically shouted the last word, "when this happened." He held up his right hand to show her the blood streaks across his fingers.

Sophia grimaced and said "Ouch." She

crossed the short space between the doorway and the twin-sized bed to look at Chance's head where the cat's sharp claws had ripped the tender flesh. A spot about the size of a quarter showed short hairs that were usually blond were now red. It looked as if a bull's-eye had been stamped on the side of his head. Seeing her kid brother, who was built like a miniature football linebacker, was still in the mismatched shorts and T-shirt he had worn at dinner the night before prompted her to ask, "How late did you stay up playing Forza with Cole?" She also saw the jewel case for the video game atop the old green-colored plastic storage container he used as a night stand.

"I don't know," muttered Chance, but he did. He had turned off the Xbox in the family room at 2 a.m., told his best friend, Cole "later," raced up the stairs with Willy following on his heels, and had dropped onto his bed fully clothed. Seconds later he had been asleep.

Sophia's "Uh huh" told him that she didn't believe him, but it really didn't matter whether she did or didn't. She wasn't his boss.

"Mom would tell you to wash the area with antiseptic," Sophia told him as she turned to walk out of the bedroom that was smaller than any other in the house. "Bathroom. Top shelf, blue bottle." Before crossing the threshold to step back into the hallway, she scanned his room with the eye of an inspector. When she spotted a pile of clothes on the floor near the foot of his twin-sized bed, she added "It's Saturday, Chance."

"I know what day it is," he growled, but she didn't hear him because she had put the phone to her ear and said, "Still there, Sarah?"

Sarah? Oh, no, he thought. Sarah Ferguson? Chance felt his stomach twist into a knot and he groaned. The sound was loud enough to cause Sophia to turn back to look at Chance as she removed the towel wrapped around her wet hair. He was still prone, but his hands were fisted and pressed into his eyes like rolled socks stuffed into gym shoes. She decided he was fine, and continued her conversation. "What? Oh, no, he's *pur-r-r-fect*," and laughed at her play on words.

Hearing Sophia's last word had him groaning again. Wasn't it just his luck—bad luck—that Sarah Ferguson had been on the other end of the open line, listening to everything that had been said, and had heard him yell out when Willy attacked. Sarah was a self-proclaimed "social media rock star" and used Facebook and Twitter to spread stories like his grandfather spread fertilizer around his precious rose bushes. Like the fertilizer, most of Sarah's stories stunk. By the start of school on Monday, everyone would know about the cat attack and his humiliation.

Chance wanted to return to his dream and to claim the trophy that belonged to him for winning the race. He lay quietly, eyes tightly closed, and asked himself, Should I go back to sleep or should I get up?, and then gently touched the side of his head with a single fingertip and felt pain. Sighing, he jumped out of bed and ran to the bathroom to search for the blue bottle of antiseptic.

SATURDAY, 8:30 A.M.

Twenty minutes later, Chance, wearing his trademark mismatched shorts and T-shirt and smelling lightly of lavender soap and antiseptic, marched barefoot into the kitchen. The room, now the largest in the house, had begun life as a narrow enclosed porch painted a dull green with a row of aging appliances on one side, and a sink and a breakfast counter covered in old, cracking Formica on the other side. His parents had spent nearly two years remodeling and expanding the area and had used recovered materials where possible. Now the room was mostly white with a stainless steel sink and appliances and butcher-block counters. There were cabinets built from wood siding recovered from an old barn, and the wood floor had been rescued from an old hotel scheduled for demolition.

A long pine table dominated the room. Twelve chairs of assorted sizes, colors, and styles were pulled up to the table. The one thing they had in common was that they all were made from wood. Seven-year-old Molly, her short dark hair pulled into pig tails that stuck out the side of her head like the brushes Sophia used to paint her face, sat alone at the table. It wasn't unusual for Molly to be sitting alone, occupied in some solitary activity.

Molly was spooning cereal into her mouth with her right hand and using the No. 2 pencil in her left hand to write on a lined, letter-sized yellow notepad. His mom had explained that Molly, the youngest of his three sisters, was ambidextrous. He wondered, as he had many times before, what it would be like to be able to use both hands to do things. In the privacy of his room he had tried several times to write his name with both hands and failed. Finally, he accepted the

THE SHOULD I? GAME

fact that, like his mother, he could only write with his left hand.

Chance pulled a chipped, ceramic red bowl out of the lower shelf of a cupboard, and grabbed the nearly empty box of Cheerios that sat on the countertop. He winced when he saw the six-inch burn ring from the hot saucepan he had placed on it two weeks before. His parents hadn't been upset about the burn ring that marred the countertop, but they had been very unhappy with his actions, which they deemed unsafe, that led to its being there. The accident resulted in his being restricted—until further notice said his mother—from cooking any food on the stovetop without supervision. When he rolled his eyes at the punishment, his father responded to twelve-year-old Chance's show of contempt by banning him from using the Xbox for two weeks. It was the worst punishment that could have been levied against Chance and no amount of pleading had changed his father's mind. Thankfully, the restriction had ended last night.

Chance filled the bowl with Cheerios,

smacking the end of the box to coax out all the cereal. Molly, who sat facing the counter, watched him pick up the O's that had escaped the bowl and pop them into his mouth.

"It's Saturday," Molly announced while she swung her thin little legs back and forth. Well-worn flip-flops dangled from tiny feet. Her attention remained divided between the notepad and her cereal bowl.

"I know it's Saturday," he said in an exasperated tone. Why did everyone keep telling him what day it was?

He had thrown his sheets and clothes into the washing machine in the laundry room before walking into the kitchen. Aside from general family chores like washing dishes, sweeping floors, dusting, and taking out the trash, each family member—except Molly who got help with her chores—had to wash and fold their own clothes, wash their sheets and blankets, make their beds, and keep their personal space clean. They were tasks that Chance sometimes found challenging.

Many of his friends didn't have the family chores he did, and some thought his parents were mean for making him share in those chores and to do his own laundry. Most of the time Chance didn't agree with his friends, but he did wish he had not chosen Saturday morning to take care of his personal chores because he had to wait until chores were done to go play with those friends. He knew he couldn't renegotiate doing chores, but he decided that he wanted to try to renegotiate when he had to do them.

For the first time since he had come downstairs, Chance spied Willy on the wide sill of the large bay window that provided a view of the patio and back yard. He looked at the cat through narrowed eyes. Willy had taken possession of a six-inch space on the windowsill between two bright red Martha Washington geraniums. Chance knew they were Martha Washington geraniums because those, and Apple Blossom geraniums, were his mother's favorites. As if sensing Chance's eyes on him, Willy turned toward him, briefly made eye contact, and then extended one hind leg skyward, splayed his toes, and began bathing himself. Chance would later tell Cole, "I swear, Willy sneered at me like Dr. Seuss's Grinch."

Chance turned and opened the door to the refrigerator, looking for the plastic half-gallon container of whole milk he had watched his mother put in there the night before.

"Where is it?" Chance called back to Molly, as he moved food items around on the top wire shelf, and muttered "Yuck" when he found a small bowl of blueberries that seemed to be growing a fuzzy, greenish-gray beard at the back of the shelf.

Molly said, "Where is what?" scooping another spoonful of milk-soaked rice cereal into her mouth.

The refrigerator door was slammed shut, rattling some oversized bowls stacked on top of it. Chance froze. When nothing fell, he sighed in relief, and turned back toward the counter and gave Molly a baleful look.

"The milk, Molly. Where's the milk?"

"Gone," Molly said casually, concentrating on eating the last bite of her breakfast.

"Gone?" demanded Chance, clutching his head between his hands in a show of frustration, and then winced when his fingers grazed the spot where Willy had attacked. What else was going to happen today!

"Gone where? I need milk for my cereal."

Molly wiggled her small body off the chair, grabbed her cereal bowl, and handed it to Chance, saying "Here."

Chance looked into Molly's bowl, scowled, and emitted a sound that was a cross between a snort and a growl. Flecks of rice cereal floated on the top. The milk was no longer white; it was a light brown. Worse, there was barely enough milk to coat his treasured Cheerios.

Molly grinned broadly in response to his reaction.

"Oh, brother," said Chance with a shake of his head. Desperate, he poured Molly's leftover milk into his cereal bowl. He was hungry. Last night he had been so anxious to play on the Xbox that he had eaten little of his favorite pasta with marinara sauce and his dad's meatballs.

"Oh, brother, what?" asked Sophia as she strolled into the kitchen. The bling phone was tucked snugly in the single back pocket of her blue-jean shorts.

"There's no milk," said Chance in an accusatory tone as he eyed the bowl Sophia held in her right hand and the spoon in her left.

Sophia peered into his cereal bowl and declared, "You have milk."

"No," he corrected her, "I have Molly's leftover milk."

Sophia lifted one of her perfectly arched eyebrows and said smoothly, "You want mine?" and gave Chance what he thought was a sly smile.

"I want my own!" he said in a huff, and used his right foot to hook the back leg of one of the chairs at the table. Once he had pulled the chair away from the table, he sat down close to Molly with a plunk. Chance wasn't thin like his sisters. He was built like his dad—solid.

On his last birthday his grandfather had showed him an old colored photograph of a short, husky boy hanging by his hands from the lower limb of a huge tree. "That's your dad at twelve," his grandfather told him, "You are the spittin' image of your dad."

Chance examined the picture and agreed. He did look like his dad at that age. The same fair skin and fair hair cut short, the same oval-shaped face with the narrow nose, and yes, the same plumb cheeks that his grandmother grabbed as if they were handles before she drew him toward her and planted a kiss on his broad forehead.

Dragging the chair away from the table drew criticism from Sophia, who sat down opposite him. "You wouldn't do that if Mom was here." He had been reprimanded on several occasions for the action. His mother told him that dragging the chair across the old wooden floor could scratch its surface, but hadn't he heard her say that little scratches and dings gave wood character? Chance sighed and thought once again how tough it was being a boy with only sisters and being the second from the youngest in the family.

"And if you wanted milk for your cereal,

then you should have been down earlier," announced Sophia in an I-know-better-than-you tone that Chance despised. "I've been up since 7 a.m." She looked at the clock that hung on the wall nearest the door to the laundry room. It was now nearly 9 a.m.

"Molly and I would have shared what milk was left in the container after Hannah and Mom and Dad took some." Without waiting for Chance to object, Sophia quickly stood up, reached across the table, and poured the milk remaining in her bowl into his. Sophia didn't have to reach far. Her arms were long, her legs even longer. At five foot six, she was a foot taller than Chance. Of course, both Sophia and Chance towered over Molly who was barely three foot seven.

Chance recoiled as if Sophia had slapped him and the spoon that was halfway to his mouth dropped in the bowl with a clang. "Disgusting," he said, and then a minute later began eating the Cheerios. Sophia laughed, and because she had, Molly did too.

"Don't you need to go to work?" Chance

asked Sophia, hoping she would say yes. Sophia worked part-time at a local coffee shop every other Saturday and sometimes during the week after school.

"Not today," answered Sophia. The owners of Java Inn had generously given her the day off as a belated birthday gift.

Sophia picked up her new phone and grinned, clearly amused by something she read on the screen. She began texting, thumbs flying across the touch keypad while Molly used the pencil to write her name and the name of her two sisters over and over again on the yellow notepad.

When Sophia had entered the kitchen, she saw the letter-sized tablet lying on the table in front of Molly and knew her little sister had been practicing her penmanship. Upon hearing that schools planned to eliminate teaching cursive writing, her father had declared that every one of his children would be able to write, to sign their name in cursive. "After all," her father, who cared deeply about education, had remarked, "no one can be assured of access to electricity, to Wi-Fi, to a tablet, or a PC. There will always be paper and pen." Since his declaration, Molly was rarely seen without a pad and a pencil.

As Chance ate his Cheerios, he watched Molly writing, puzzled by what he saw.

His light brown eyebrows knit in a frown, Chance asked Molly, "How come you're not writing down my name?"

Molly, her face expressionless, shrugged her narrow shoulders, continued to write, and said without looking up, "You're a boy."

Disturbed by her answer, Chance threw back "So?" in a less than friendly tone.

Sophia immediately stopped typing a message on her cell phone when she heard Chance's question. A week ago she had been sitting on the floor in the bedroom she shared with Molly, digging around in the closet for a particular pair of sandals and overheard a conversation between her parents about Chance. Her mother had told her father she suspected that their little boy sometimes might feel like he was on the outside, despite their efforts to balance family, social, and sport activities that included everyone. After all,

THE SHOULD I? GAME

her mother explained, the girls were at different life stages. "You mean they're more and more involved in *girlie-girl* activities," stated her father. There had been no verbal response from her mother, but Sophia imagined her smiling and nodding in agreement. She did, however, hear her mother suggest that they needed to involve Chance in activities whenever they could. It was her father's turn to agree and added, "Except when he's grounded." Her mother had laughed at the comment.

Sophia put down her phone, pointed to Molly's list, and said, "Look, Chance. Molly has written down a color next to each name."

Chance leaned over to look more closely at the list. As Sophia had said, there were colors written next to each name.

"They're nail polish colors," Sophia explained. She swung sideways in her chair, lifted her right leg into the air, and wiggled her toes to show off her toenails. "Hot Flamingo Pink," she told him.

Molly had written pink next to Sophia's name, except she had replaced the 'i' with an exclamation mark. P!nk was a rock star whose music their mother liked. Chance knew that Sophia secretly listened to some of the explicit versions of P!nk's music, which their mother had forbidden her to do. He was holding on to that bit of knowledge just in case.

"Molly, show Chance your feet." At Sophia's direction Molly kicked off her flip flops, twisted in her chair, and practically shoved her tiny feet into Chance's face to show him toenails that were painted a neon orange color. He shrank back in the chair, partly because her action caught him off guard and partly because he thought the neon orange color on her toenails was really ugly.

Molly flung back her head and giggled at Chance's reaction. "Orange Posh." She continued waving her feet in Chance's face until he pushed them away, which only made Molly giggle more.

"Splash," corrected Sophia, who thought the name was ridiculous, but didn't say so. "Orange Beach Splash."

Ugly color, ugly name thought Chance.

Molly asked Chance if he wanted a color

added next to his name. She used her fingers to count and call out the available colors. "Black as Midnight, Orange Beach Splash, Firefly Red, Seaside Blue, Hot Flamingo Pink, Raging Purple, and Fresh Moss Green. Seven colors."

As he often did when hearing something he didn't like, Chance curled his upper lip. "No way."

Without interrupting her texting, Sophia told him, "There are male rock stars who wear nail polish."

He answered with "The only time I'd wear nail polish..." and then paused. He was about to tell them he'd have to be a corpse before he would let anyone put some hideous polish on his nails. Instead he said, "The only time that I *might* think about wearing paint on my nails is Halloween."

With that concession, Sophia told Molly to add Chance to her list and to write down the colors black and green next to his name followed by October 31. Molly rocked in the chair and giggled, and then carefully wrote down the information, misspelling October.

Any further discussion about the list was interrupted by a very loud and very popular hip hop ringtone that came from Sophia's cell phone. Once again, Sophia tapped the screen and began typing. Willy, startled by that sound or some other noise, leapt off the windowsill and ran out of the room.

It was Chance's turn to call out rules, and he took a slight pleasure in doing so. "Mom and Dad said the phone was off limits when you're not alone." Sophia slowly raised her head, and glared at him with sapphire blue eyes so bright and intense that they looked like glowing laser beams.

Their father wanted people to "talk to each other face to face" so when Sophia was presented with the phone a new rule was put in place. It was a simple rule. No texting and no talking on a cell phone when there were two or more people present in a communal space.

Not surprisingly, Sophia had stiffened and asked, "What is your definition of communal space?"

It was their mother who answered

Sophia between sips of tea. She rattled off the names of areas she considered off limits. "The kitchen and living room, family room, front porch, patio, and..." she paused, 'the car. Any place, Sophia, where there are two or more people present. And one of those people would be you. Got it?"

Sophia objected to what she called "an incredibly unfair rule." Chance and Molly, both of whom were deemed by their parents to be too young to have cell phones, were silent.

The question about usage hadn't come up until Sophia got her phone. Hannah was his eldest sister and she had had a cell phone for two years.

Hannah stepped into the discussion. "Staying connected is important, especially if making arrangements for a sports event, a social event, a last minute change to a work schedule, a news flash about weather, traffic, school. And then there is the most basic reason—an emergency."

Their parents listened and when Hannah quit talking their father said, "All reasonable circumstances, Hannah. Your mother and I will discuss it and let you know in the morning." And they did. After breakfast the next day, their mother told Hannah and Sophia, "You can set your phone on vibrate when we are gathered as we now are, but I do not expect anyone to instantly respond to a call or a text message unless it is an emergency. And then," and she looked directly at Sophia, "depending on where you are, you will excuse yourself. Too many 'excuse me while I answer this' and we'll take your phone."

Hannah, pleased with the compromise, had said "Thank you." Sophia was slower to say thank you, unmistakably unhappy with her parents answer. She was, by far, the more social member of the family and frequently tied up the land line, something that annoyed everyone.

Chance once had asked Hannah, "How come everybody wants to talk to Sophia? Is it because people think she's pretty?" He had noticed when they went out together that people often stopped and stared at Sophia.

Without hesitation Hannah said, "It's her personality. Sophia is friendly and nice to everyone."

Confused by the response, Chance had said, "Aren't you?" Hannah had laughed and said she was, but not to the same degree as Sophia. This statement drew yet another question from Chance. "What does that mean?"

Hannah took her time answering his question. "It just means that I'm more of an introvert. Sophia is an extrovert." Before Chance could ask for an explanation, Hannah held up her hand signaling him to wait. She strolled out of the room, and shortly thereafter strolled back in and handed Chance a used hardcover edition of the American Heritage College dictionary. "Look'em up, bro." Hannah spelled both words for him and left him to learn the meanings. It was that day that Chance learned that he, like Hannah, was an introvert.

Chance ignored the ugly look Sophia now gave him and asked, "Where are Mom and Dad?" Even before she answered, he remembered they had told everyone the night before what their agenda was for the next morning. It was routine for the family to share schedules at dinner time.

As Sophia answered Chance's question, Molly once again kicked off her flip flops and scurried barefoot out of the kitchen.

"Mom is walking with Cole's mother, and Dad is in the garage with Mr. Jones. I think Dad is working on some do-whacky on Mr. Jones' old car." Chance was guessing that his mom and Mrs. Wykowski could be anywhere within a two-mile radius. From where Chance sat, his dad was just five feet away in the detached garage, which was just out of view.

For the first time that morning, Chance smiled broadly and gleefully grabbed the opportunity to correct his sister. "The do-whacky is the starter."

"Whatever," said a disinterested Sophia a minute before Molly skipped into the room clutching a pair of anklet socks in each hand.

"Red? Blue?" Molly asked, pumping her arms in the air and waving the socks as if they were miniature flags.

To Chance, Molly looked like a bobble head doll. Her head rotated from side to side and then up and down. He rolled his eyes at the sight of the socks. Sophia saw the eye roll, extended her right leg under the table, and nudged him with her foot. He protested by calling out "Hey" and glared at her.

"Who cares," he said grumpily. He wore plaid shorts that were clean but a little wrinkled, and a striped short-sleeve T-shirt that was frayed around the neck and had a few holes along the hem. Soon he would dig his feet into well-worn Vans—without socks. Unlike his sisters, he didn't care what he wore. He took a final bite of cereal and wondered what Cole was doing.

Molly frowned at Chance's reaction. Sophia, who was busy finger-combing long, naturally curly red hair that framed her heart-shaped face, said absently, "Molly, are you playing Should I?"

When Molly nodded yes, Sophia, who was wearing a tangerine-colored tank top with a flower design that complemented the blue-jean shorts, said, "How do we say it, Molly?"

"Should I wear red socks or should I wear blue?" Molly said excitedly, laying the socks on the table next to the yellow notepad.

Sophia reached across the table, picked up the socks, and displayed each pair by holding them on either side of her lightly freckled face. Chance noticed that one of Sophia's fingernails was painted the same hideous color as Molly's toenails. Weird he thought.

Molly flung back her head and giggled. "I choose blue."

"Yes, you do," Sophia laughed. "Blue kind of matches your butterfly." Molly was wearing her favorite pink T-shirt with a big multicolored butterfly that was faded because it had been laundered so many times. At one time the butterfly had been bright blues and pinks. Sophia was acknowledged by everyone as the family "fashionista" and tried to gently guide— never push—Molly in her clothing selections. Molly's current wardrobe choice was uniquely hers, and not one Sophia had pointed her toward.

Molly jumped off the chair and ran around the table to snatch the blue socks from Sophia's left hand.

"Why do you want to wear socks?" snarled Chance. "It's seventy-six degrees outside. You don't need socks. Just wear your flip flops."

Molly reacted immediately to Chance's flippant tone, the question, and the comment. She lifted her chin defiantly, purposefully turned and faced him, and showed him the whites of her eyes. It was a new facial expression and he wondered where she had picked it up.

Weeks earlier he had spied Molly in the upstairs bathroom, standing barefoot on a battered red, wooden step stool, hands braced on either side of the sink, and leaning toward the wall-mounted mirror. Her mouth was opened wide and her lips were stretched across her teeth. Because her toothbrush and a package of dental floss were on the counter, he thought Molly was simply trying to see if there was something caught in her teeth. Minutes later that thought was squashed when he realized that she was practicing different facial expressions.

Curious, he stood quietly and watched her squint, wrinkle her nose, stick out her lower lip, and take her face through a variety of smiles, frowns, and pouts. When she tried to add audio by growling, he laughed. Molly's attempt at a fierce growl sounded more like the squeak of one of Willy's mouse toys. Startled, Molly had turned and glared at him, her round face flushed with a mixture of embarrassment and anger. She jumped off the stool and stuck out her tongue at him before slamming the door in his face.

Now Chance answered her eye roll with a forced grin, teeth clenched. Geez, he couldn't wait to get outside. Remembering his sheets and clothes were in the washing machine, he ran into the laundry room to put them in the dryer, successfully escaping being drawn into playing the game.

"Your turn," Molly told Sophia, ignoring Chance's hasty departure.

Sophia quickly surveyed the room, trying to decide what she could use, and then spied the fruit in the big ceramic bowl with brightly colored stripes that sat permanently on the counter. "Should I eat an apple or should I eat an orange?"

"You choose," cooed Molly.

"I'll have an apple," answered Sophia.

Molly grabbed an apple from the bowl and handed it to Sophia.

Sophia smiled, said, "Thanks, Molly," and looked first at the Honeycrisp apple, and then at Chance who had just reentered the kitchen. She really didn't want the apple, so she just sat it on the table in front of her.

HELEN R. LETTS

SATURDAY, 9 A.M.

Chance was rinsing out his cereal bowl and was about to place it in the dishwasher when he heard the front door open. He turned to see Hannah, his oldest sister, walk into the kitchen and he smiled. From her outfit of gray shorts and white tank top with a big orange swoosh across the front, and sports shoes with orange ankle socks, it was clear she was returning from a run.

Hannah, according to Sophia, was a natural beauty with her cream-colored skin, high cheekbones, and full lips. Sophia believed Hannah should be modeling sports clothing; Hannah disagreed. Chance did think his sister was much prettier than many of the girls on the glossy cover of sports magazines.

Hannah strode over, wrapped her arms around him from behind, and hugged him tightly. She swung him gently from side to side and kissed him lightly on the top of his head before she released him and moved toward the table. Hannah bent down and wrapped her arms around Molly, who answered the embrace with a giggle. "What are you doing, Molly?"

"Playing," said Molly, showing eighteen-year-old Hannah the blue socks on her feet and the red socks on the table.

Removing a pistachio-colored hair tie that secured her long, thick, straight black hair in a ponytail at the top of her head, Hannah asked, "Should I?" even though she knew the answer. Hannah's hair fell down her back almost to her waist.

"Yes," answered Sophia, tucking her hair behind her ears, showing the tiny silver hoop earrings that had been a birthday gift from Hannah. Because Molly was distracted, Sophia quietly got up and returned the apple to the bowl.

Hannah turned her attention to

Chance, who had reclaimed his seat at the table. She could see light shadows under his eyes and suspected he had probably stayed up far too late playing a game on Xbox. "How about you, Chance? Are you playing?'

Chance stopped gazing at the sunshine outside and looked at the sister he adored. She was a star basketball player in her senior year of high school who made time to shoot hoops with him at least once a week. And he liked the fact that the older boys at school were always nice to him because he was "Hurricane" Hannah's little brother. Basketball and track were her things and she excelled at both. She jumped and ran as if there were wings on her feet; each move seemed so effortless, so easy, so right.

Chance sighed and said "I wasn't."

"C'mon," said Hannah, nudging him gently by pressing a fist into his upper arm and giving him a light push.

Hannah didn't hear Chance's answer, distracted when Jake Bowker, her boyfriend of six months, walked into the room, jangling car keys. Behind Jake was his best friend, Kelly Jones. She dashed past both Jake and Kelly to close the front door she had left open for them and was not surprised to see Willy sitting just inside the living room to the right of the door. She was grateful that the cat's own sense of security prevented him from darting outside.

Sophia, who secretly had a crush on Kelly, sat up a little straighter and pulled her hair out from behind her ears. To her knowledge, it was the first time Kelly had been in their house. Both young men were members of the school's track team, and both were what their paternal grandmother, who had attended several track meets, described as "the proverbial tall, dark, and handsome." Their mom had translated the statement. "She means they are really good looking." The girls had wholeheartedly agreed with the assessment.

Both boys were tall—Kelly was about six foot and Jake was an inch shorter. Both had black hair. Jake's was wavy and hung to his earlobes, while Kelly's was short, cropped, and curly. Both had great smiles, wonderful personalities, and, given the fact both were stars on the school's track team, surprisingly small egos.

Hannah's parents liked Jake. Her father, the day after Jake had joined her family for a Saturday afternoon of grilled hotdogs—or tube steak as their grandfather called them—and vegetables stated, "I like that young man. A good package of brains and brawn." From her father, that was a great endorsement and Hannah had beamed knowing her father approved of her current choice of a boyfriend. Her mother had expressed her approval at the close of the evening with a simple "I like him."

In their own rights, Jake and Kelly were high achievers, tearing up the track at remarkable speeds, most often challenging the records of past athletes. But, if you asked them, it wasn't so much about breaking someone else's record, it was about surpassing a goal they set for themselves.

Sophia greeted Jake and Kelly with a smile and a cheerful hello. Hannah sat down beside her and introduced Kelly to

Chance and Molly. Jake said hello to everyone, and then turned and asked Chance how he was doing. Chance answered "good" and knew he would stay and play the Should I? game as long as Hannah and Jake were present.

It was Kelly's first time in Hannah's house and he looked around the kitchen with interest. It was clean and tidy but clearly lived in. It also was casual, inviting, and obviously designed to unite the family for meals and other events and he liked it instantly. He especially liked the built-in desk that provided a home for a computer and assorted books and papers. It looked like the desk in his own small bedroom and the familiarity made him smile.

He walked over to a wall decorated with black and white photographs. All were dressed in brightly colored frames. He took a minute to look at the pictures. They showed the Newbold family engaged in different settings from the beach to the mountains. He particularly enjoyed one of the larger photographs. Every member of the family was standing in the kitchen

THE SHOULD I? GAME

that looked much different than it did now and was wearing a hard hat, goggles, and a smile.

"Play, Chance," Hannah said in a playful tone, her right hand resting lightly on his shoulder. He would do most anything for the sister he remembered reading to him, playing trucks with him, teaching him how to skateboard, and helping him to learn how to read and write. Chance discovered he liked to write stories. It wasn't something he shouted out to his friends and only Hannah had read them.

Before Chance could answer, Jake asked "Play what?" as he rinsed sand off the bottom of a bottle of orange juice.

Molly's young shrill voice rang out. "Should I?"

Kelly Jones, who propped his large, lean frame against one end of the kitchen counter, said "Never heard of it."

"I hadn't either until five and a half months ago," Jake told him as he bent over and rubbed the calf of one leg that felt tight from the run. "If you spend any time in the Newbold house, there's a good chance you'll learn about the game." He had been introduced to the game months before at a Friday pizza night with Hannah's family.

"It's pretty simple," Jake told Kelly. Then he said, "Should I stand up or should I sit down?"

Automatically the Newbold children said in unison, "You choose." Kelly raised his eyebrows, finding the group response a little strange.

"I'll sit," said Jake, claiming the red enameled chair opposite Chance and Molly and placing the juice bottle on the table.

Chance called out, "Should I play inside or should I play outside?" There was a chorus of "You choose." He really wanted to be practicing some freestyle maneuvers with his skateboard. All he needed to do was run up to his room, grab his bicycle helmet, wrist guards, and board, and go to the skatepark. And he needed to call Cole. He tossed the idea around in his head, and then decided he'd wait.

Chance said, "For now, I'll play inside."

Kelly threw up his hands in surrender, saying, "Okay. I get it. I've got one. Should

THE SHOULD I? GAME

I stay or should I go?"

"You choose," everyone answered.

"So what's the point?" Kelly asked, thinking the game was rather silly. "You pose a question about choices, but the choice always falls back on the person who posed the question."

"Exactly," said Hannah, stretching an arm across the back of Chance's chair. Hannah's fingernails, unlike Sophia's and Molly's, were not polished.

Jake, who had been rolling Molly's pencil between a thumb and index finger, spoke up with "That is the point. It's about choices."

"I get that," Kelly answered in a tone that clearly said "duh."

"There's more to it than a simple this or that," Jake told him, rubbing the back of his neck and then stretching it first left and then right.

"It's about actions and accountability," added Hannah, who was looking at Sophia's nail polish and wondering why one fingernail was painted an awful orange color.

"And responsibility," Sophia interjected.

"And consequences," piped up Chance.

"And rewards," chimed in Molly, who was still busy writing.

"Guys," Kelly started, grabbing the edge of the counter with both hands. "We make choices all the time. What am I missing?"

"You're right," acknowledged Hannah. "We do make choices all the time. Some choices are routine, automatic. Should I get up or should I stay in bed? Should I wash my hair today or should I wait until tomorrow? Should I drink a glass of water or should I drink a can of soda?"

"Pretty simple," responded Kelly.

"Somewhat," answered Hannah, drawing out the word. "Everything we do is about choices, and the accountability and consequences for those choices. Sometimes your choice involves only yourself. Often your choices involve others. When we make choices that affect others, we take on even more responsibility. "

She paused, about to add something, when Chance spoke up.

"And it's thinking...really thinking," he said with a determination in his voice that caught even Hannah off guard, "about why you choose to do what you do. Dad told me to ask myself what the...what was his word..." he struggled to find the word. Seconds passed before he grabbed the memory of his conversation with his dad and exclaimed, "Payoff! That was it, payoff. What is the payoff for the choice you make?"

Hannah tugged at Chance's left earlobe, her finger rolling over the tiny mole that had appeared there several years before. Others might interpret the action as mean, but he knew what it was. It was a sign of approval from his older sister.

Jake, seeing that Hannah was about to say something, raised his index finger as if he was going to reach out and press pause for audio. "Your dad is right, Chance. You do have to ask yourself what the payoff is. Another way to look at it is to simply ask yourself, 'Why am I doing this?' In other words, what is your motivation?" Jake wasn't just repeating what he had heard on many occasions from his own parents. He believed what he was saying.

Hannah, her expression sober, added,

"There are choices that aren't straightforward. Some choices demand that you think about what you are going to do or not do, and to ask yourself what the benefit is—to you, to others—for making that choice."

"Okay," said Kelly. "But sometimes there are no clear-cut choices." Kelly was thinking back to a bad choice his older brother, John, had made years before when his family had called home a city hundreds of miles north of where they currently lived. His brother's offense was simply being a passenger in a car driven by a young man who had been drinking. At the time, John had no other way to get home from a party that was miles from their house, so he had hitched a ride. Unfortunately, the driver missed a hairpin turn and crashed the car into a tree. Fortunately, the only body severely damaged belonged to the family's Subaru Forrester he had been driving. All five human bodies in the car were intact, although there were scrapes and bruises, a ticket, a court date, and a really big fine for the driver, the much older sibling of one of John's closest friends. And the price of John's decision to accept a ride, even though he hadn't been drinking, cost him his position on the football team in his senior year of high school even though he had passed a breathalyzer test. His parents objected vehemently to the school's decision and so did most people in the community, but in the end it simply didn't matter. The school dismissed his defense, pointing out that it had—without exception—a zero-tolerance policy with substance abuse. So John became a casualty of the rule and, Kelly supposed, his own actions. John made a bad decision, and because he had, the dreams John had for his senior year fell flat. Fortunately, it was the police record of having zero alcohol in his system that allowed him to persuade the college that had offered him a football scholarship and then withdrew it, to reinstate it. It was a hard lesson for John. And it became a lesson for Kelly as well.

"You're right," said Sophia without hesitation. "People who have limited resources to housing, food, clothing, education, money, and guidance have few choices. In their lives there may be only one option or none at all."

"And you're right," said Kelly echoing her initial response. He looked at Sophia with new eyes. He and Jake had never talked about Hannah's younger sister, but he had heard others make remarks about her. Sophia was pretty, very pretty, but in some circles at school she had a reputation as being social *and* shallow. He reserved judgment about people until he got to know them personally. Social didn't bother him, but shallow did. He deliberately didn't hang with shallow people. Her statement made him think that her being tagged as shallow might be unjustified.

Continuing, Sophia said, "And how we think is a choice. You can choose to be happy or you can choose to be sad. You know, the choice between negative and positive thinking."

Kelly, Hannah, and Jake said, "Absolutely" in rapid succession. Chance just sat like a sponge and absorbed the exchanges and Molly continued to write, seemingly oblivious to the conversations unfolding around her.

Sophia, who had observed Kelly's interest in the bowl of fruit on the counter, said, "So, Kelly, the question that may be going through your mind right now is, Should I ask if I can have some fruit, or should I not ask at all?"

"Wow," said Kelly, flashing Sophia a big, slightly crooked smile that displayed his dimples. "Are you psychic? That's exactly what I was thinking."

"Help yourself," a grinning Sophia told him, and Kelly said "thanks" and reached over and grabbed a large orange from a striped bowl.

Hannah joined Kelly behind the counter and handed him a paper towel that he could place the orange peels on.

"Would you like some fruit?" she asked Jake, who had turned his head to look at her. She held up an orange and an apple. When he pointed to the apple, she rinsed it, yelled "Catch," and tossed it to him. She chose an orange for herself.

"Anyone else want some fruit?" asked Hannah, casting a look at Chance and then Molly. Both shook their heads no.

"Sophia, how about you? Some fruit?"

"No," answered Sophia, "I'm good." She had been ignoring her vibrating phone, but this time looked at who was calling. She pressed Ignore, then dropped the phone into her lap to hide her actions and quickly sent a text message. When she looked up again, Chance's eyes were fixed on her. She flicked him a look that said, "Don't you dare say a word." He didn't. But he tucked the incident away just in case.

"How about something to drink?" Hannah opened up the refrigerator and found some lemonade in a container on the top shelf. "Lemonade? Water?"

Sophia again declined the offer, but Chance indicated he would like some lemonade and chose to get it for himself. When Molly said she wanted some water, Chance offered to get it for her, asking only if she wanted it with or without ice.

Not surprisingly, Molly's response was "Should I have ice or should I not have ice?"

Everyone, including Kelly, said, "You

choose."

When she gave her answer, Chance put ice in her glass before filling it with water.

"So, Hannah, when did your family start playing this game?" asked Kelly, dropping orange peels on the paper towel Hannah had given him.

"I think I was...umm, twelve," said Hannah, brows wrinkled as tried to recall how old she had been when she started playing the Should I? game.

"I remember playing it with you," said Sophia, ignoring her vibrating cell phone. She had turned off the ring when she saw Kelly enter. "Wasn't there a neighbor..."

"Yeah, there was," filled in Hannah, and recalled the girl who had lived in the house next door for just over a year. "Her name was Sharon."

"Yes. I remember now," Sophia exclaimed. "Sharon Lawrence." And then almost as an afterthought said, "She was mean."

"Yes, she was," agreed Hannah. "She used to sneak up behind people..."

"Me," said Sophia while stealing a glance at her vibrating phone.

"Me, too," said Chance.

"And me," said Hannah. "And she would push them to the ground."

"Sounds like she was a bully," Jake said.

"Sounds like my cousin, Charlie," Kelly stated. Charlie really was a bully who had finally stopped pushing Kelly when Kelly pushed him back one day and said, "Don't do it again." Of course, at the time Kelly had grown to be a foot taller and 20 pounds heavier than Charlie.

"She was a bully," confirmed Hannah, "At the time we just thought Sharon was incredibly mean. A real pest. But Mom and Dad thought there was a reason she wanted to hurt people."

Jake looked at her quizzically and asked what he thought was an obvious question. "Did they think someone was hurting her?" Hannah gave him a sharp look. She had wondered after Sharon was gone if that was the reason for her bad behavior, but at the time such a thought would never have crossed her mind.

"I don't know. Maybe," Hannah said sadly. "There was an older brother that

THE SHOULD I? GAME

called her 'a little fatty'. Sometimes at night you could hear shouting coming from the house and you could hear Sharon crying."

"Did you avoid her?" Kelly wanted to know.

Hannah turned and looked at him directly. 'No. Mom and Dad told us to say, 'Thank you, Sharon, for being my friend', each time she made us a target."

Amazed, Jake asked, "How did that work out?"

"It took time, but eventually she quit the sneak attacks, quit pushing us to the ground, and really did become a friend."

Kelly said, "Really?" at the unexpected answer. Jake was equally surprised. "She became your friend?"

Hannah smiled and nodded yes. Sophia added, "We played together, had meals together. There was never a sleepover, but yeah, she became a friend."

"For a year," said Hannah, looking to Sophia for confirmation. "And I remember that she lost weight. Then we came home from school one day and learned that her family was moving to another state. We just lost touch with each other."

"So it was because of Sharon that you started playing the game?" said Kelly, eating his final orange segment.

"No, not Sharon," said Hannah.

"Who?" Kelly asked. "Your mom? Your dad?"

"Actually," Hannah told him, "I think it was Aunt Becca that started the game."

"Is Aunt Becca your father's sister or your mother's sister?" Kelly wanted to know.

"Our mother's sister," responded Sophia.

Jake shifted in the chair to look squarely at Kelly. He had taken a seat that had him facing the backyard. "You know their Aunt Becca," he said with confidence.

A frowning Kelly answered. "I don't think so."

"Yes, you do," Jake declared. "Aunt Becca is Mrs. Bastion, our English teacher."

A wide-eyed and astonished Kelly blurted out, "But she's black!"

Jake instantly choked on the orange

juice he had just taken a drink of. Sophia and Chance just looked at Kelly dumbfounded, and Molly started shouting, "Aunt Becca is black" over and over and stopped only when Hannah silenced her with a gentle tug of a pig tail and a simple "Shhh, Molly."

It was Hannah, in her usual calm, who responded to Kelly's statement, "Yes. She is black. So are you."

Everyone laughed.

Kelly, who shook his head and dropped his chin to his chest in embarrassment, said in his own defense, "My parents are black, yours are white."

Jake raised his eyebrows. Pretending offense, he pressed his hand over his heart and said, "And I tell people you're my brother."

"And everyone knows that you say that because of a certain..." Kelly was trying to find the right word, still choking mentally on his show of social ineptitude.

"Kinship?" suggested Hannah with a smile.

"That's it," Kelly gave Hannah a thumbs up. "Kinship."

Hannah explained, "Aunt Becca and our mother are sisters. Both were adopted."

"I'm adopted," piped in Molly. Given the fact that Molly unmistakably was of Asian ancestry, the news surprised neither Jake nor Kelly. Hannah's announcement did.

"I'm adopted and part Native American."

The news took Jake by surprise and he stopped drumming his fingers on the table. He could say only "Wow." Kelly uttered a low "Cool."

"We're a blended family," Chance stated proudly, "And Mom and Dad love us equally."

Hannah beamed at her little brother, "Yes, Chance, we are loved."

Jake stared across the table at Hannah, brown eyes meeting brown eyes, and said, "You didn't tell me you were adopted."

Hannah's answer was unguarded and without malice. "I didn't think it was important. I think of myself as the eldest daughter of Thomas and Mary Newbold, and the sister of Sophia, Chance, and Molly Newbold."

Jake was about to comment that the issue wasn't the fact she was adopted, but about the fact she hadn't shared she was adopted, and then realized it was her business, not his, and that it really didn't matter. Hannah was, well, Hannah, and she was wonderful.

"And the niece of Mrs. Rebecca Bastion," Kelly added as he wrapped up the orange peels in the paper towel. He appeared to be looking for the garbage can when Sophia explained, "The peels go into our compost bin."

She got up and extended her hand to him. "I'll take them."

"We have a compost bin because we grow vegetables," Molly informed Kelly, who watched Sophia deposit the orange peels and core of the apple Jake had eaten into a small plastic bin that sat on the countertop to the right of the sink.

"Impressive," Kelly said sincerely, and then asked, "What do you grow?"

"Tomatoes, zucchini, and string beans," Molly said, who had reclaimed her pencil and was writing on her notepad.

"And what else?" Hannah prompted.

Molly lifted her head and stared at Hannah, a look of puzzlement on her face.

"Po-o-o...," started Hannah.

"Oh, yes," squealed Molly. "And we grow potatoes."

The conversation about vegetables ended with Kelly uttering a simple, "Nice," and Jake saying "And I can confirm that they're all really tasty. Raw, steamed, or grilled." Most of the vegetables his parent's served with meals came out of a box or a bag that lived in the freezer. He made a mental note to talk to his parents about starting a small vegetable garden in their backyard.

SATURDAY, 9:30 A.M.

Kelly turned the conversation back to the subject of the Should I? game.

"Do you know why your Aunt Becca created the game?" he asked, finally taking a seat at the table. Completely relaxed, he stretched out one leg and leaned an elbow on the table.

Stepping into the kitchen, Hannah took the lead on the explanation.

"No, not really," said Hannah. "We just started playing it one night when Aunt Becca and Uncle Taylor were visiting and it just stuck. It was fun so we just kept playing."

"As I said earlier, we started playing when I was about twelve. So six years ago." She turned on the faucet with the water filter and refilled her glass. "That means Sophia would have been ten, and Chance was six. Molly wasn't yet a member of the Newbold clan."

She paused and asked if anyone else wanted water or needed a refill. After handing a glass to Jake and Kelly, she continued. "A few years later...which would make it about four years ago I suppose...Aunt Becca showed up one evening. She was very upset. I remember only because we were having dinner and she burst into the kitchen, sobbing...I guess you would say uncontrollably. It scared me. She said one of her students had nearly died in an accident and the incident made her unhappy. Mom shuffled Aunt Becca out of the kitchen. Dad gave us really big bowls of ice cream and then he joined them. Uncle Taylor showed up much later in the evening."

"Oh," said Sophia excitedly. "I remember that. It was scary."

"Do you know who it was that nearly died?" said Kelly.

"What?" answered Hannah, her lips

pursed as she concentrated on trying to recover a memory. "No. Not really. But I think it was a boy. Someone named Kim or Jim or Tim. Something like that. I don't remember."

Jake's head snapped up. His mother had a distant cousin named Julia who had a son named Tim that had almost died about four years ago in an incident at Tim's school. It couldn't possibly be the same boy. This was probably some really strange coincidence because of the timing and the similarity with the name.

"Are you sure," questioned Jake, slightly anxious. "I mean, are you sure the boy's name was Tim."

"Well, not absolutely. Sorry. Why?"

"I know this is totally off the wall, but my mom's distant cousin has a boy named Tim that nearly died about four years ago."

Surprised, Hannah said, "What?"

"Tim was playing and fell into a pond and would have drowned if a teacher had not reacted quickly, at least that's what I think happened. I don't recall the details. I just remember his mom crying and saying that no one was helping him and that the teacher saved his life," Jake told them. He also revealed he had met Tim Gray only once at a family reunion when they were children. Both his mother and Tim's mother shared the same great grandfather. "Tim has CMT."

"What's that?" asked Chance.

Jake turned his head toward his left shoulder and twisted his mouth as if doing so would result in his spitting out the right answer. "I think it's some tooth disease. I only remember it because it is the same abbreviation of Country Music Television." That admission got everyone's attention, and he explained, "No, no. Not me. Dad watches that channel sometimes. I like country music, but I..."

"Do you need a shovel, Jake?" Kelly asked and then mimicked the motion of digging a hole.

"Let's look it up," suggested Sophia, as she stood up and placed her cell phone in her back pocket. She marched over to the computer, sat down, typed in a password, and searched the term CMT, adding the word disease. She got over a million hits. She opened the link to a Mayo Clinic article, scanned the page, and started reporting her findings.

"There's a Charcot-Marie-Tooth disease. That's a CMT abbreviation. I probably just mispronounced it but there's no audio attached to the page to give me the correct pronunciation." She paused, glanced over her shoulder, and gave Jake a look of concern. "It's a group of hereditary disorders that damage the nerves in your arms and legs."

"I do remember my mom saying Tim fell a lot," stated Jake.

Having clicked the link to the symptoms page, Sophia called back. "Yes, it's one of the symptoms. Frequent tripping or falling."

"And there's no cure," Jake said, which Sophia confirmed minutes later as she read through the content on the treatments page. He recalled that years before he and his mom had looked up the disease on the Internet.

Hannah instantly thought back to some recent occurrences of Jake tripping or stumbling when they were running together. Had it been coincidence or something else entirely? She queried him about the hereditary aspects of the disease. Seeing the concern in Hannah's eyes, Jake reached across the table and squeezed her hand to reassure her. The personal display of affection, a spontaneous gesture, made Molly giggle. It was hard not to smile when Molly giggled because it was so infectious. Nearly everyone, except Sophia, who was still at the computer, smiled.

Kelly faced his best friend. His voice had the same concern that he had detected in Hannah's voice. "Really, Jake. Do you need to worry?"

"No," Jake assured them both. His elbows were propped on the table and his hands clasped together. Hannah could see that he was no longer in the Newbold House at 342 Cherry Lane, but somewhere far away. Jake suddenly felt guilty. He hadn't thought about Tim in years. At last he said, "The disease is on Tim's father's side of the family, so I have no worries there."

"Could Tim have been one of Mrs. Bastion's students?" Kelly said.

THE SHOULD I? GAME

"I don't know," Hannah said. "Aunt Becca made the shift to teaching high-school English about three years ago. She used to teach at Washington Middle School. That's about two hours from here."

Sophia, who had been cruising through links announced, "There's an article—it's cached—about a Tim Gray." She had quickly read the page and excitedly called out, "Yes. Tim had been a student at Washington. She scrolled down and hit another article, saying, "Creepy" when she silently read its contents. Sophia's reaction was instant. So was her revulsion.

Her reaction piqued everyone's curiosity. "What does it say?" asked Jake, who had propped his forehead against his clasped hands. Sophia was reluctant to read it aloud and motioned Hannah over.

Hannah read it, briefly shifted her attention to Molly and Chance, and then told Sophia to print it.

Chance had said little, and Molly nothing at all. Hannah was grateful that Molly seemed absorbed in writing on her yellow pad because Hannah wasn't sure

63

that her parents would approve of Molly's presence when there was talk about a child that had come close to dying years before, regardless of the reason. In three weeks Chance would officially be a teenager so she thought his presence was not inappropriate. But Molly was a different case. Hannah asked her, "What are you writing, Molly?"

Chance had been overseeing Molly's writing as the discussion about the game, Aunt Becca, and Tim Gray unfolded. It looked to him like Molly was making out lists for a party, a fact that Hannah confirmed when she looked at it minutes later.

"Are we all invited to your party?" Hannah asked Molly.

"Yes," said Molly without looking up. "It's a barbeque."

The printer spit out a single page. Sophia quickly reread it and handed it to Hannah.

"So read it aloud already," said Jake. Clearly Hannah was hesitating. He held out his hand for the page. It took only a quick scan to understand why neither

THE SHOULD I? GAME

Sophia nor Hannah wanted to read the article out loud. It wasn't a news article though. It was more of an excerpt, like something that might be part of an official record—like a police report—and he wondered how it how managed to live so long as a cached page on the Internet. He looked at the URL and it was one he didn't recognize, but then he thought, why would I? I only use the Internet when I must for research.

Fearing he was about to be excluded, Chance said, "Hey, I want to read it."

Hannah and Jake looked at each other.

"Molly," Hannah said with a deliberate smile, "would you go to my room and find my sandals with the rhinestones—you know, the sparkles—along the straps?"

Molly quit writing, lifted her head, tilted it to one side, and gave Hannah a long, assessing look. "Yes, but I could have just covered my ears." Then without another word, she once again wriggled off the chair and left the room.

Jake waited until he could no longer hear the slap of Molly's flip flops on the wooden stairs, and then asked Sophia to

65

read the printed page aloud.

"They claimed they had simply been teasing Tim and that his falling into the pond was an accident. They were playing at the pond—which really was little more than a swampy area—next to the school playground. One of the boy's had attached a rope to the branch of a nearby tree and all were taking turns pretending they were swinging across the Copper River from one large outcrop of rock to another by using a rope. They used the rope to get a running start and leaped from one side of the pond to the other. Tim had been watching them for some time when one or more of the boy's suggested that Tim join in the fun. When it was Tim's turn he made several false starts, falling, getting up, and starting again. On the fifth try he managed to get some height and was swinging across the pond when he just let go of the rope. He fell into the water, face down, and nearly drowned. A teacher, having observed this play and the participants, had been moving toward the boys to stop it. She was alarmed when she saw Tim had been pulled into the

THE SHOULD I? GAME

game. When she saw Tim fall she shouted to another teacher to call 911."

"Oh my gosh," said Sophia. Hannah looked stricken by the news, but was silent. Jake's face was rigid; his eyes were downcast and focused on some invisible spot on the table. Kelly sat stiffly, waiting patiently for Sophia to continue, while Chance looked from one person to the next, noting their facial expressions.

Sophia took a deep breath and then continued. "According to the teacher, when Tim fell face down into the water, all of the boys just stood there laughing, making no effort to help him. When questioned, each boy—Randall Simmons, John Petrovyn, Jordan Jacobs, Michael Walker—said they didn't realize Tim was in trouble. Their answer seemed innocent enough until the teacher explained that the same four boys had repeatedly engaged in activities designed to taunt Tim, challenging him to participate in physical activities that they were well aware he was incapable of doing. It was her belief that they had bullied Tim into joining them in the game knowing full well

67

he would fall." Sophia's voice had grown raspy and she paused to take a sip of water from the glass Hannah handed her. "She further believed that their failure to assist the boy when he fell in the water would have led to his death if she had not been there. The teacher was distraught and kept repeating that she felt responsible for not taking a more proactive role in addressing the bullying before."

Minutes after Sophia read the last sentence Kelly said "Harsh."

"Extremely harsh," muttered Hannah and Sophia echoed her words. Jake and Chance remained silent.

Frowning, Kelly said, "It almost sounds as though they wanted him *not* to get up."

Sophia dropped the sheet of paper, print side down, on the table. The very idea that one person wanted to hurt another for any reason sent chills down her back. Someone wanting to hurt another person because they thought it would be fun made her physically ill.

With a subtle shake of his head, Jake said in a low voice, "It does read like that doesn't it."

THE SHOULD I? GAME

Kelly said, "Sure does." When no one else spoke he said, "These kids were what, twelve, thirteen back then?" He looked at Chance. "That's about your age isn't it, Chance?"

Chance, who was still processing what Sophia had just read, could only nod yes.

Jake cut in, "For the fun of it," the note of disgust in his voice unmistakable. "Isn't that what we hear about similar incidents today, that they did it for the fun of it?"

Hannah said, "Sadly, yes. Do we ever really learn the reasons for terrible acts of violence?" She thought back to the violent acts, many carried out by young people, that had occurred the past few years across the country and felt immense sadness.

Looking directly at Jake, Hannah asked, "Had you ever heard this story before?"

"No," Jake answered. And why would he have heard the story. It was four years ago and he had been fourteen. His parents—at least then—would have shielded him from the truth. Shifting his gaze to Hannah, he asked, "How about you? Do you think it was your Aunt Becca that saved Tim?"

Hannah shook her head vigorously, "I honestly don't know. I find it curious that they name the boys but not the teacher."

"Well," cut in Sophia, "we do know Aunt Becca taught at Washington six years ago. She was teaching there when she and Uncle Taylor introduced us to the game."

"If this is a connection, it is one that I never ever, ever expected," Hannah said, feeling slightly distressed by these revelations.

"How is Tim, Jake?" asked Kelly with genuine concern. "Do you know?"

"I don't," admitted Jake. "I think his family moved to another state shortly after that incident."

If anything else was to be said it wasn't because Molly reentered the kitchen and handed Hannah the sandals she had been sent to retrieve. Hannah thanked Molly and placed the sandals on the floor next to her chair.

Sophia said, "It's very sad. If it was Aunt Becca that saved Tim, then we now know why she started the game."

Chance agreed. "Yeah."

"She once said she started the game

THE SHOULD I? GAME

because she wanted to help kids stop and think about their actions," Hannah said.

"That would be my take," Jake said.

Sophia added, "Aunt Becca is always saying that life is like a gigantic map. The direction you go, the place you land, is up to you."

Sophia's words brought a smile to Kelly's face.

"She says that in class. Often," Kelly told her, and he had thought about the path he wanted to take in life.

"Does she also tell you to not let anyone steal who you are and that it's okay to be different?" asked Hannah.

"Not exactly in those words," answered Kelly. "I've heard her say that gardens are most beautiful, most interesting, when filled with different flowers and plants."

Sophia smiled, "That sounds like Aunt Becca."

"I started playing the game with my little brother, Caleb, and sister, Cate," said Jake. "We've talked about choices. I want to help them to understand that every action, every decision, has a consequence. Good or bad."

Delighted with this news, Hannah clapped her hands together and exclaimed, "That's wonderful, Jake."

"Yes, it is," Kelly said, now thinking about who he could introduce the game to.

"Speaking of consequence," said Hannah. "Can we keep this piece about Tim to ourselves?"

"Works for me," said Jake.

"Me, too," said Kelly, and then Chance added his agreement.

Everyone turned their attention to Sophia.

She looked slightly offended. "Well, of course. Why hurt people."

"Sarah Ferguson is your best friend," Chance declared, thinking about the cat attack that already could be headlining her blog today. "She writes things to get attention. Mean things. It's cyber bullying."

No one was shocked by the accusation. It was the fact that it was Chance that made the accusation that was most shocking. Sarah, who admittedly had no athletic talents, in the past year alone had managed to write something derogatory

THE SHOULD I? GAME

about Kelly, Jake, and Hannah and their athletic skills.

"She's a friend," Sophia said defensively. "She is *not* my best friend."

Hannah intervened with "Best friend or not, Sophia, you must admit that Sarah does write things that hurt people. The story about Tim Gray and a possible connection to Aunt Becca needs to remain where it belongs—here, in our house, and in the past."

Her face now pink, Sophia said forcefully, "She will not hear it from me."

One by one, each person pledged, "Nor me." Molly alone said nothing. But then, Molly, or so they thought, didn't know what they were talking about.

HELEN R. LETTS

SATURDAY, 10 A.M.

There was an awkward silence that followed, one that Kelly broke when he said, "Wow. That was a pretty serious conversation." He stopped talking just long enough to remove his cell phone from the pocket of his shorts to check the time. "Yeah," he continued. "A heavy topic for a Saturday morning."

There was a coolness in Jake's retort. "What are you saying? That serious conversations should be reserved for, what, afternoons and evenings?"

Recognizing disapproval in his friend's tone, Kelly assured him with, "No. It's just not a conversation that I expected to have."

Hannah said, "I think we need to have more conversations about bullying."

Jake sighed deeply. His voice was still tight when he said, "Yes, we do."

Sophia, Chance, and Molly said nothing.

Kelly stood and said, "I promised my mom I'd help her set up tables for a community potluck at the senior center this afternoon."

Jake looked up at him. "So we need to go now?"

"Pretty much," said Kelly, "unless you want me to take your car and you can catch a ride home with Hannah."

Jake pushed back his chair and stood up. "Nah," he said. "I need to get home and take a shower. I think my mom volunteered me to help with that same potluck set up."

"And I have to go work for four hours at the Sports Shack," said Hannah as she double checked the time by looking at the wall clock. She had about an hour before she was expected to be behind the counter helping customers. "And I definitely need to shower."

As Hannah, Jake, and Kelly were exiting the kitchen, Sophia called out, "It was nice seeing you, Jake." To Kelly she said, "Come again, Kelly. Any time."

Chance simply said good-bye and Molly lifted her arms in the air and used both hands to wave farewell.

Hannah walked Jake to the door, and everyone could hear him say that he would pick her up at 7 p.m. for the beach party, and heard Hannah counter with 7:30. They also heard Jake greet Mrs. Newbold and Mrs. Wykowski, Cole's mom, and Hannah introducing Kelly to both women.

Anxious to be outside, Chance ran into the laundry room and quickly removed and cleaned the lint vent. He pulled out his laundry, and scooted pass his mom and Mrs. Wykowski with a hello and balled up sheets and clothes. He needed to call Cole before he made his bed and folded his clothes. Willy, who had remained sitting in the living room, watching the entries and exits, raced up the stairs after Chance.

Sophia was also making her escape. As

the two women entered the kitchen, she said, "Hi, Mom. Hello, Mrs. Wykowski. Gotta run. I'm meeting Krystal and Ellen at the Java Inn." Before she could hear their greetings, she was out the door, her phone to her ear.

Only Molly remained in the kitchen, sitting quietly and contentedly at the long table, writing on her yellow tablet.

Turning to her youngest daughter, Mrs. Newbold pulled back her shoulder length, dark red hair and secured it with the pistachio-colored hair tie she found lying on the counter. "So, Molly, what have you been doing?"

"Playing," answered Molly.

"Playing what?"

"Should I?"

Puzzled, Mrs. Wykowski asked, "Should you what, Molly?"

"It's a game," Molly's mom told her. "The Should I? game."

"Never heard of it," Cole's mother said.

Genuinely surprised by the answer, Mary Newbold said "Really?" as she put the tea kettle on. "Cole plays it with Chance and us all the time."

THE SHOULD I? GAME

Emma Wykowski reiterated that Cole had never introduced her to the game.

Mary walked over to the table, pulled out a chair and pointed to it. "Have a seat, Emma, and I'll tell you about the Should I? game over a nice cup of tea."

HELEN R. LETTS

Newbold Family
Should I? List

These are just some of the Should I? questions that Hannah, Sophia, Chance, and Molly have produced over the last four years. Some are routine, but some are not. Some need to be followed by the question why, and some do not. Create your own Should I? list.

Should I accept the criticism or should I reject it?

Should I accept the opinion or should I reject it?

Should I agree or should I not agree?

Should I ask permission to use this or should I just use it?

Should I be a follower or should I be a leader?

Should I be a friend or should I be a foe?

Should I be a participant or should I be an observer?

Should I be good or should I be bad?

Should I be kind or should I be mean?

Should I be naughty or should I be nice?

Should I be polite or should I be rude?

Should I be silent or should I speak out?

Should I be the voice of change or should I change my voice?

Should I be weak or should I be strong?

Should I believe what I'm told or should I question what I'm told?

Should I choose an apple or should I choose a pear?

THE SHOULD I? GAME

Should I choose red or should I choose blue?

Should I choose round or should I choose square?

Should I climb the stairs or should I ride the elevator?

Should I drink this or should I drink that?

Should I eat this or should I eat that?

Should I express my opinion or should I keep it to myself?

Should I express gratitude or should I withhold it?

Should I follow my instincts or should I dismiss them?

Should I follow or should I lead?

Should I give someone praise or should I give them criticism?

Should I go left or should I go right?

Should I help or should I not help?

Should I keep my promise to help or should I break the promise?

Should I listen or should I not listen?

Should I live in faith or should I live in fear?

Should I live to please others or live to please myself?

Should I look up or should I look down?

Should I make a cake or should I make a pie?

Should I ride my bike or should I ride my long board?

Should I tell someone what I think I heard or should I not tell someone what I think I heard?

Should I tell someone what I think I saw or should I not tell someone what I think I saw?

Should I play this or should I play that?

Should I pretend to understand or should I admit that I don't understand?

Should I read this book or should I read that book?

Should I return what I found or should I keep what I found?

THE SHOULD I? GAME

Should I say hello or should I say good-bye?

Should I say let's stay or should I say let's go?

Should I say yes or should I say no?

Should I seek the positive or should I give in to the negative?

Should I share or should I not share?

Should I smile or should I frown?

Should I stand up or should I sit down?

Should I succeed or should I fail?

Should I take responsibility for my actions or should I not take responsibility for my actions?

Should I tell the truth or should I lie?

Should I travel by train or should I travel by plane?

Should I treat you as a friend or should I treat you as a foe?

Should I volunteer or should I not volunteer?

Should I walk or should I run?

Should I watch this TV show/movie or should I watch that TV show/movie?

Should I wear this or should I wear that?

ABOUT THE AUTHOR

Helen R. Letts is the author of the *What's behind the curtain?* series of peek-a-boo books illustrated by Sandie Hawkins. Helen lives in the Pacific Northwest and is a technical writer/editor in the software industry.

MY SHOULD I?

~or~

~or~

HELEN R. LETTS

~or~

~or~

THE SHOULD I? GAME

~or~

~or~

HELEN R. LETTS

~or~

~or~

THE SHOULD I? GAME

~or~

~or~

HELEN R. LETTS

~or~

~or~

THE SHOULD I? GAME

~or~

~or~

HELEN R. LETTS

~or~

~or~

THE SHOULD I? GAME

~or~

~or~

HELEN R. LETTS

~or~

~or~

THE SHOULD I? GAME

~or~

~or~

HELEN R. LETTS

~or~

~or~

THE SHOULD I? GAME

~or~

~or~

HELEN R. LETTS

~or~

~or~

THE SHOULD I? GAME

~or~

~or~

HELEN R. LETTS

~or~

~or~

THE SHOULD I? GAME

~or~

~or~

HELEN R. LETTS

~or~

~or~

THE SHOULD I? GAME

~or~

~or~

HELEN R. LETTS

~or~

~or~

THE SHOULD I? GAME

~or~

~or~

HELEN R. LETTS

~or~

~or~

THE SHOULD I? GAME

~or~

~or~

HELEN R. LETTS

~or~

~or~

HELEN R. LETTS